RUMORS OF MARTY GOODE

Jeff Ryan Williams

MOON
FORTRESS
PRESS

CONTENTS

RUMORS OF
MARTY GOODE

LATE NOVEMBER 2013

I WATCH AS WE BEGIN our nighttime descent, my brow and cheekbone against the plexiglass, trying to make sense of the reddish-orange grid below, the endless streets and buildings, the cars. I imagine each of them en route to someplace of consequence.

We are passing through a hazy middle, the ceiling of clouds above us holding the same unnatural tint as the city below. I watch as we turn, the great white wing tilting down quickly toward the expressways, the factories and warehouses, the great swaths of retail. We level out, the landscape still generic, undistinguished, more of the same, schools and ballfields, high-rises, office buildings and apartments, the geometric collections of public housing, their sad uniformity.

I watch, becoming restless, anxious, searching the endless flow of landscape, trying to identify the familiar, the comfort of shapes I know. They are rushing by, the streets and buildings, endless, unfamiliar, innumerable, a massive backlit lattice. And then, the surprise of a sudden curving darkness: it is a river, the Hudson.

And there it is, distinct and unmistakable, Lower Manhattan, an immediate contradiction, the dark outlines of unlit office towers silhouetted against glimmering avenues, the skyscrapers crammed tight. It occurs to me that it all looks fake, impossible, like an architect's scale model, which is what makes it all so magnificent; it is real.

We bank left, turning north on final approach, then level out again. The East River directly below, the bridges pass beneath us one by one, the city flattening out just north of downtown, the low-lying neighborhoods, a brief display of modesty lasting three, maybe four seconds before midtown begins to rise, the clustered skyscrapers, the white frenzied haze above Times Square, the bright galactic center, absurd, even from this distance. Like a glimpse into another dimension, it seems almost unreal. And then, as if in recompense for the preceding blaze, the dark void of Central Park easing into view, that blank corridor, the vast negative space.

The interior cabin lights click on.

We touch down at LaGuardia three minutes later, a little before eight on Sunday evening. I text my son Wade as we taxi to the gate, then sit, waiting, watching as the other passengers gather their things, row by row; the slow deboard.

"I'm walking out now," I say fifteen minutes later, stepping into the chilled air, looking for a black Audi. I spot him a couple hundred feet down, and we maneuver our way toward one another. Wade jumps out of the car, gives me a hug and puts my luggage in the trunk. It's been about six months since we've been together.

I pull the passenger door shut, a muffled thump, and we're off. The ride is smooth, almost silent.

"This is nice," I say.

"I'm glad you decided to come, Dad."

The roads are busy, full of cars. It's 9:30 by the time we reach his apartment—he moved here in in August—a three-bedroom overlooking the Hudson. We stay up late, talking, catching up. It's nearly midnight when I brush my teeth.

Monday morning we walk to breakfast before his first appointment, and then the day is mine. The museums and the park, the restaurants and shops, the new memorial downtown. Three days to explore, to wander, to relax. Each night we meet up for dinner.

I was eager for the trip, the change of scenery, my time with Wade, but still, it isn't the same without her. I miss her, my best friend. I catch myself, again and again, wanting to comment to her, to say, "Look at that; see how it's changed?" or "Remember that time?" and so on. I realize I am lonely. I realize I am alone. But maybe I'm not alone: Maybe her spirit is here in these streets alongside me, quiet but strong. It's a comforting thought, although the truth is I don't feel anything.

Wednesday evening Wade and I walk over to a Thai place just around the corner, a cramped, eclectic space in the basement of an old Catholic School. Pork satay, chicken curry puffs, squash dumplings; then dessert of creamy coconut ice cream served right out of half-shells.

Later that night we sit bundled on his balcony talking, the river hidden in darkness before us, the nickel-sized orbs of our cigars blooming and receding in the night.

"So you think the real estate market's really coming back?" I ask.

"It's killer, Dad. If this deal closes next week, it'll be my ninth this year; almost one per month. I'm number three in the office."

"I'm proud of you, son—all your hard work. I wish your mom could see this."

"I know she can."

"Right," I say, tugging at my coat zipper. "I suppose you're right." The wind is picking up, the temperature dropping. I let my mind drift out into the darkness.

"I can't wait for tomorrow," Wade says a couple minutes later.

"My surprise, right?"

"You won't believe it."

FIVE-A.M. ALARM; SWEATPANTS, HAT, GLOVES; morning walk, the huddled crowds lining Broadway, out early for the parade. A glimpse of SpongeBob, distended, drifting sideways down Central Park West. Coffee, toast, three pieces of bacon, extra crispy. Then I'm back at his apartment by eight o'clock, ready to go.

Wade eases the car to the end of 72nd Street, then guns it onto the Henry Hudson, my weight pressing into the heated leather seat. Out my window the naked trees of Riverside Park and the city rush past, 79th, 92nd, 125th, the traffic thin because of the holiday. We're soon up and over the George Washington Bridge, pushing north again, the Palisades, the speedometer rubbing ninety. I cross my arms, breathe deep and wonder what awaits.

FALL OF 1960

Life is a series of images.

A line of cars along either side of the road, Fords and Chevys. Children playing on a trampoline, the fitful, uneven bounces up, down, high, higher, giving the mothers fright. The homemade ice cream machines churning, a half-dozen, at least, taking what seemed like forever. And the celebrated man, walking tall and proud through a crowd thick with people gathered just for him.

The house sat at the end of Frenchtown Road. I was seventeen and there for the beer. Actually, I was there for Brenda Carter. It was her uncle's party. He was turning forty, which was a big deal in those days. Everyone showed up.

Father Parry made his way over to our group, his yellow, jagged grin creeping me out as he surveyed each of us, his eyes bouncing along from face to face until he settled on me.

"Tom," he said, "your mother says you're giving real thought to seminary."

"Maybe," I said. "Not sure yet."

"I still remember our visit. You were four or five, asking about the apocalyptic stories in the Revelation." He glanced down at the bottle by my side, taking a drag from his cigarette. "You had questions about the moon turning into blood. 'Only red *like* blood,' I assured you." Father Parry breathed out smoke as he said this.

It was an all-day kind of party. Burgers, hotdogs, and a gathering mass of rival potato salads. Bobby Rydell and Connie Francis on the radio, the adults preoccupied with the election, who looked better on the TV? Which of them was best to deal with the Russians? We sat around wide wooden tables eating, talking, making fun of one another. And I kept my eyes on Brenda, thinking of the clever things I might say.

Then came the cool autumn evening, the sun slipping into the trees, and the smell of wood smoke in the air. The birthday cake was cut, the ice cream was ready. People began to make their way around the side of the house, gathering out back. We followed the girls, finding a spot to sit on the cold grass.

Soon, he stepped up onto the old, broad stump, the celebrated man, steadying himself with an old axe, the same one the children had used in vain throughout the day to try and leave their mark upon the remnant of oak.

And then he spoke. His words pouring out warm and effortless, like the voice of some radio god.

"Thank you. And I mean it. Thank you, everybody. Thanks for being here. It means a lot. Some of you know the men in my family ain't known for our longevity. Neither of my granddaddies saw thirty-five. My papa drowned when we was little. And his brothers, my uncles; well, Paul killed his self with a pistol and—oh, shit! Aunt Clara, I'm sorry."

He laughed, made a face.

"And the war got the rest, the younger ones, Johnny, James. God bless. So I guess I feel like some kinda goddamned Methuselah or something, making forty. You all know I was over there too, and there's just one reason I'm here today."

He let this hang out there for a moment.

"And his name is Marty Goode. God bless Marty Goode."

"Tell it," someone shouted from the darkness. "Tell your story."

"Go on," another yelled out.

"Yeah, so some of you've heard this before, but it's a good one I suppose. August 9, 1943, and we're headed home from a mission.

"Our target had been a ball bearing factory forty miles outside Berlin. I'm a waist gunner on a B-17, and we're limping along, having taken flak and lost both port engines. This was before the P-51 escorts, and we're lagging behind the squadron. Still, the crew's in high spirits. The raid was a success, with no casualties on board, which is always a good day.

"And while that's all great and good, we're over the English Channel when two Focke-Wulf 190s catch us. The lucky bastards get our tail gunner, Jimmy, almost immediately. Me and Pete Danno, the other waist gunner, we do our best to hold them off, but on the third or fourth pass they strafe the hell out of the cockpit, and the whole bird pitches left. Right away I feel us losing speed and altitude. 'Oh, Jesus!' I say to Jesus, and I'm thinking the nose must've caught fire or something, 'cause then the whole cabin starts to fill up with smoke. I'm struggling with my gear, trying to get free, but the fall's got me pinned against the frame. I say to myself, *this is it*.

"Then suddenly, the plane eases up a bit, and I'm close to getting my feet. And then, bap, bap, bap, the Luftwaffe strafe us again. This time, a round must've hit a hydraulic pump or something, 'cause the next thing I know I've got a face full of hot grease, and I can't see a goddamned thing. But I hear these words, like a voice or something, but not a normal voice, and then something brushes past me. Then more talking, and I feel my face being wiped clean, real soft, gentle, like maybe a mama would a child, you know?

"And I open my eyes, and what do you know, there he is, Marty, our bombardier, grinning at me. He'd been a professor at some university in Baltimore, but he'd signed up to fight the Nazis, and anyway, he's cleaning me up, helping me get free, saying, 'Don't you worry, friend, everything's gonna be all right.' This crazy guy, his flight suit is half burnt up and he says, 'Look,' and he points out at a couple of RAF Spitfires racing past us to intercept the Germans. Anyway, they must've bought us some time, 'cause it takes a couple minutes for Marty to get the parachute on me, and for him to lead us to the rear hatch.

"'I'm right behind you,' he says. I'll never forget, my eyes locked onto his as he shoved me out. Those eyes, they were special eyes, like from another world or something. I'd never noticed that before. And then, not two seconds after I'm clear, my eyes still locked on his, there's a flash, an explosion inside the plane, little pieces coming off, fire and smoke out every hatch, even though the bird's mostly still intact. My chute catches, and I watch the bomber drift, rolling slowly away from me, then down and over, twisting, falling, spinning toward the earth, a suspension of black smoke hanging behind.

"I watched 'til it hit the ground. I could see four other chutes below me. I touched down in a cow pasture a couple miles inland and eventually made my way back to the shoreline, where I met up with the crew. Turned out Marty, God bless him, helped each one of them get clear. The rest—Jimmy, our tail gunner; Harold, our pilot; Leon, the copilot; and Glen, our radio operator—all got killed in the strafing. They never found Marty's body. Probably blown clear in the explosion, they said, although I sure didn't see nothing like that."

He paused for a moment, the crowd rapt in the darkness, then he raised a beer in the air.

"And so I say, God bless, Marty Goode. My guardian angel. God bless you, Marty, wherever you are. You're the reason I'm here tonight."

IT WAS A CUTE STORY, and with an epic as broad as WWII you heard a lot of heartwarming tales of heroism, the war now distant enough for most folks to find some nostalgia in it. But sitting there, listening, it was the date of the event that stuck with me most. August 9, 1943, the day I was born.

SEPTEMBER 1968

THINGS NEVER WENT ANYWHERE with Brenda Carter, but I did meet Patti Perkins at that party.

Five years later, Patti and I honeymooned in Hilton Head. I was flipping through a book I'd brought, she was in the shower, and the television was on. The volume was low, some program about mysteries of the English countryside. Fairies and Stonehenge, cattle sacrifice and crop circles, that kind of thing. I happened to glance up as the camera was zooming in on a yellowed calendar, a date circled in heavy red ink. August 9, 1943. I eased off the bed and walked across the room, twisting up the volume.

A reporter was interviewing an old man, a farmer, who, on the highlighted date, had been out tending sheep on his property when he had heard the purr of aircraft.

A voiceover explained:

The sound was common, daily, as his acreage was flung across the flight path linking London and Berlin. The curiosity was one of hardware and markings. Half an hour earlier he'd seen a squadron of Allied bombers heading home, and only minutes prior he'd witnessed two RAF fighters roaring toward the channel.

The camera focused on the old man's eyes, now wide.

"And then I saw the smoke."

A thick black cord curling across blue sky, the failing bomber inverted, the terror of gravity, an eternal minute, and then a shock of light and sound just beyond the tree line, the ground trembling beneath his feet.

A bright orange fireball rose into a swirl of black. He arrived within a couple of minutes, heart pounding, lungs heaving, expecting to find the wreckage spewed over a few hundred meters. Instead, he found a gaping hole in the earth.

"I didn't know what to do with myself. Knowing there could be no survivors, I decided to sit myself down under a tree, rolling cigarettes to ease my nerves, trying to decide."

The air blurry with heat, he considered the situation for nearly two hours, waiting as the fire burned itself out, the black crumpled wreckage eventually becoming visible. And then it occurred.

"I was beginning to wonder about the sheep when I heard it. This banging. Kind of a bang, bang, bang, you know? I walk over and look down into the hole, the best I could with the heat and all, the shell still smoldering, the air like a furnace, my eyes burning. And then a panel of the fuselage pops open, falls to the side, and—I still can't believe it—this figure emerges, pushing his way out of the hull, ribbons of smoke swirling all around him. I think I probably dirtied myself."

The farmer watched as a man climbed his way out of the cavity, focused and naked. And completely unscathed. His skin pink and smooth.

"He had very nice hair, I remember. Walked right up to me and asked if he could borrow my trousers . . . and maybe my shirt. I obliged him, still in shock. He thanked me, then walked right off into the forest, left me standing there in my dirty underpants."

This mysterious survivor was never identified, never seen again. To this day a crater can be seen in the fateful spot where the bomber smashed into the earth. This farmer, now close to sixty years old, says some days he still finds himself back at the same spot, wondering how to make sense of it all. And what happened next makes us all consider, are there things in this world we don't yet understand?

There was a closing shot of the old farmer explaining what happened next.

"Maybe two weeks later, this salesman from the city shows up, says he's from Harrods, takes all my measurements, then leaves without explanation. A month after that seven trunks arrive: shirts, suits, pants, socks, neckties, gloves, coats, shoes, boots, belts, hats, pajamas. Even a dozen pair of new undershorts. All a bit too fancy for my taste, but the underwear was nice. And I had no doubts: immediately I knew it was from *him*."

"What are you watching, Tom?"

I glanced up, startled, the trance broken. It was Patti, standing in the door frame, radiant in the blue dress she'd found earlier that day in one of the shops, her dark hair falling past her freckled face, her skin bronzed from the sun.

"I'm not really sure," I said, my head still swimming.

MAY 1973

EVEN SINCE CHILDHOOD I've felt it, a persistent restlessness, a sense of lack, despite my surroundings. At times I felt guilt; why couldn't I just be content like everyone else? Was there something wrong with me that I so often found myself unfulfilled? Or maybe it was nothing more than a little boredom. Maybe I just expected more from the world than I was getting? And then it would always happen, the next sudden surprise to propel me forward.

I WAS THIRTY, and we were at a faculty party. Patti was now working at the university and we were new to town, trying to make friends.

Around midnight I was in the den, tired and ready to go, sitting across from the host, a religious studies professor named Ray Kruppold. He was telling stories, sipping sherry. His chance meeting with C.S. Lewis after the war. His thoughts on Tolkien's elves, ideas on Melchizedek, the legend of the wandering Jew. He said his pet hobby was immortality.

"We just don't seem to want to die, do we?" he said, with a grin.

"I guess not," I said.

"My favorite tittle-tattle," Professor Kruppold continued, "is that of John of Patmos."

I nodded, weary.

"You're familiar?" he asked.

"No," I said.

"There was gossip of it, even during the time of Jesus of Nazareth."

I tried to focus.

"Stories that one of his followers, John, would not die until Christ's return."

"I don't remember that," I said.

"Well, it's there. Jesus himself acknowledges this in one of the Gospel accounts. You can look it up. This same John is believed to have written the Revelation while in his nineties. Some traditions hold he never died, that he's still alive, still among us, even today."

I glanced toward the kitchen. Patti was leaning against the counter, talking with another woman, laughing.

"And?" I said.

The professor cracked a wide smile and leaned in toward me.

"I will show you something."

He led me toward the front of the house, through a pair of French doors and into his study. A dim corner lamp provided the only light.

"Watch your step," he said.

The room was a jumble of knee-high stacks of books and papers, magazines and journals, save a narrow channel of carpet leading through the middle to his desk. He knelt to pull open a cabinet, retrieving something, an object wrapped in a crimson velvet, which he carefully removed, revealing a half disintegrated book.

"What is it?" I asked.

"A journal," he said. "Here, let me find the piece I'm thinking of . . . alright, begin here, the part about the birds."

Gulls spotted just past dawn on this fifteenth day of June, 1649, and this sighting bringing a great relief to the ship's crew, giving their thanks to God, for the arrival of our vessel at Massachusetts is imminent.

On yesterevening the men being anxious for port sat about sharing much foolishness and laughter. My enjoyment of their stories was great until one of the men shared a tale sending a chill down the full length of my spine. It was our quartermaster who spoke of the legend of Sir Milamar of the Desert who survived the second battle of Jerusalem and due to his extreme long livedness was himself the source of an early cup legend, having been sustained in the desert for three hundred years.

Finding boldness in drink and such a late hour I asked the quartermaster whether the man which he spoke of was the Crusader known as the enlightened one?

The quartermaster looked back upon me as if struck dumb.

I continued my inquiry and asked the quartermaster again if this was the knight who fought against his own, the one who turned the Templars back. Some turned back with by words, others with his sword.

The study of men and their behaviors must be my concern moving forward, as the reason why my interjections were so unwelcome is a complete mystery to me. Perhaps it is because some men find loathing in the understanding of wisdom and sound judgment. Perhaps it is my own laziness and lack of study of the ever shifting attitudes of men. Nevertheless I shall double my own efforts to understand this present generation.

I retired to my bunk with a feeling of disheartenment and thereupon found myself reminiscing, although wrestling might be the more appropriate word, for it is true that memory is not my kindest servant and in vane I tried to recall the year I'd left for Klashna.

"What does it mean?" I asked.

"Do you know the name Klashna?" Kruppold asked.

"No, who's that?"

"It's not a *who*, it's a *where*. An ancient castle in the Slavic lands, situated between modern Bucharest and the Black Sea. The Slavs have a legend, a story of one who occupied the castle for many years, centuries they say. An immortal being who seduced their women, only their best, with stories of adventure, knights in shining armor and a faraway island called Perellia."

"Why would they allow something like that?"

"Something like what?" Kruppold asked.

"The seduction of their women?"

"Oh, well, he only took a bride every generation or so. He was supposedly a monogamous fellow."

"And the women chose him of their own free will?" I asked.

"How many women do you know? In my experience they generally all like castles and islands. So I can imagine he was one popular devil." Kruppold said this with a shrug, making a funny face. "And it's real; I've been there."

"The legend?" I asked.

Kruppold laughed. "The castle. But look at this . . ."

He grabbed a cardboard tube from the corner, fishing out a large piece of paper, a map, which he unrolled on a desk before me.

It read **_Mare Medi Terranevm_**.

"The Mediterranean Sea. And here it is," he said, his index finger tapping at a golden spec in a sea of blue. "Perellia, a tiny island, sparsely populated for millennia. And to this day the pillar's still there, a crude shrine, from the first century. There is an inscription, *et exspuens in mari*, the one spit out of the sea.

"And there is a thirteenth-century document in the Vatican archives—I know a man who's seen it—about the knight mentioned earlier, the one famous for switching sides during the Crusades, holding an outpost in the desert. Not that it stopped the Europeans, of course—water always finds its way through stone—but it did force them to other routes, the more difficult ones, the longer ones. The Muslim armies referred to him as the Saint of Perellia."

My head hurt. I looked down at the crumbling book still in my hand, trying to make sense of it all.

"These men are somehow all connected?"

Kruppold worked out a deep, congested laugh.

"A prophesy of the disciple who would not die, a first-century shrine on a deserted island, a Crusader who would not Crusade, a recluse in the wilderness of Eastern Europe, the journal of a man during his voyage to the New World? These men are more than connected, my friend. These men are all one in the same."

THE FOLLOWING AFTERNOON I was lost in thought, occupying myself in the workshop I'd built behind our house, carefully measuring the cuts. I loved the feeling, my fingertips running along the wood.

I heard a car door shut. I glanced up at the clock. It was already 5:45. I walked out to meet Patti in the driveway, gave her a hug.

"Hey, come see," I said. We walked back to the workshop.

"It's beautiful," she said. "How long will it take to finish?"

"Another couple weeks. I want to make a little chair for him, too."

"You're so sure, aren't you, that it's going to be a boy?"

"I just know," I said, pulling off my gloves and hanging them on the wall.

"Oh, so I got to work this morning and the gentleman you were talking to last night, the religion professor?, he met me at the door of my office. He was apologizing, telling me he'd had too much to drink; 'a huge embarrassment,' he said. But anyway, he asked me to tell you he was sorry."

"Sorry?"

"He said he had gotten all carried away, had told you some things, crazy stories. Tall tales, he said. He told me to tell you to please forget the whole thing."

"Really?" I said, tapping my fingers on the raw wood of the unfinished crib. "Oh, OK."

24

"OK, good," Patti said.

"Still," I said, "it was some story. I couldn't help but think of that party. Brenda Carter's uncle? That story he told at his—"

"Tom."

"No, I know, it's just that it all seems to tie together really well, you know?"

She looked right at me. I knew that smile.

"I love your imagination, honey, always have. It's just like when we first met. Everything you were into, you were so sure of it all, right?"

"Yep."

"But where did it lead?"

"Right," I said. "You're right."

"Like Dr. Kruppold said, it was just a story."

"Yes, you're right, honey. Just a silly story."

AND I MIGHT HAVE ACTUALLY DONE IT, listened to her, let it go, forgotten all about it, had the professor not mentioned a certain name as we said goodnight. The name Marty Goode.

OCTOBER 1976

PATTI WAS SO MANY THINGS: a free spirit, a light, a center of gravity; easy going, driven to achieve; uplifting but grounding; brilliant, loyal, with no tolerance for bullshit. And she was always a skeptic.

I STOOD BEFORE THE HOTEL MIRROR, buttoning my shirt.

"Is that new?" Patti asked.

"I picked it up yesterday," I said, "at Barney's."

"Barney's? That's different."

"Different?"

"For you, I mean."

"Do you like it?" I asked.

"I do. And what did you decide about today?"

"Maybe I'll walk up to the Met, not sure yet. You know how I like to wander," I said.

27

"I'm jealous. I'll be stuck in meetings all day. What a bore."

"I really miss Wade," I said.

"He'll be fine. I'm more worried about you."

She left for her conference. I went downstairs, read the paper in the lobby restaurant, and watched the door, waiting.

At half past eleven a man walked in off the street. He looked like some kind of muscle man, his thick black arms, almost cartoonish, ballooning out from his thin shirt sleeves.

He came toward me and leaned on the bar beside me, his forearms on the counter, his gaze straight ahead.

"Hello?" I said.

"You are waiting for something?" he asked, his accent was heavy, South African.

I had rehearsed the line I'd been given a hundred times.

"For the end of the world," I said.

He glanced over. His eyes were vacant.

Soon we were in a silver coupe, a convertible European make, headed north on Fifth Avenue, then cutting west across the park, then north again until we reached the George Washington.

"I'm Tom," I said, trying to project my voice over the wind noise.

He nodded.

"What's your name?" I asked.

"Abraham."

Crossing the bridge, we continued north, in New Jersey briefly before passing back across New York state lines, the Hudson visible down through the trees to our right.

"Looks so rural already," I said. "Hard to believe we're so close to the city."

Abraham didn't reply. His attention was focused on the two sleeves of rice cakes nestled between the bucket seats. Every couple minutes he pulled another of the blanched disks from the wrapper, taking intermittent sips of water from an old milk jug on the floor board.

"Such beautiful country," I said.

WE WERE NINETY MINUTES NORTH of the city, racing along a two-lane highway, thick woods on either side, the occasional mailbox or hand-painted sign, and the intervals between oncoming cars stretching out. We shot across a small bridge, and in another five hundred feet I could feel Abraham applying the brake.

Slowing to a near stop, he then eased onto a gravel drive. The rocks crunched beneath our tires as we wound deep into heavy woods, a thick canopy shading the ground. Several hundred feet in we passed beneath a stone arch, algae stained, and the iron gate rusted out, half of which was broken from its hinges and leaning against the dark pillar. Across the arch was an engraving, a fierce-looking eagle clutching an elaborate letter *J*.

We continued, the bumpy road jerking us forward and back, the tires at one point slinging rocks against the wheel wells as Abraham tried to keep us from bottoming out. In the wooded distance I spotted a tall, colorless figure, slender but pained, her marble face turned away from me. Beyond, there were others. A half-mile from the main road the trees began to thin, sunlight breaking through in spots, and I could see it now, just ahead, some kind of sprawling structure.

Abraham pulled the car beneath a stand-alone shelter, a simple construction, sheets of rutted steel draped across a half-dozen cast-iron poles. We parked between two other vehicles—an olive Plymouth sedan and an old pick-up truck, both its back tires flat. The road beyond this point was dug out, an excavation a few feet deep and several hundred feet in length. A bulldozer sat idle on one side, weeds pushing up out of the heavy scoop of dirt held high in the air.

"This way," Abraham said.

I followed him along the edge of the trough, dead leaves underfoot. I'd been fine in the convertible, but now I noticed a chill in the early afternoon air. A pair of squirrels darted back and forth through the underbrush, up and down tree trunks, chasing, playing.

We passed through a crumbling wall, once waist high, the pitted surface white with bird droppings. Now I could see the estate; the size was shocking. Three and four stories high, an imperishable mass, thick and stony at its core, its serpentine extensions splaying out, then coiling back on themselves to form courtyards and gardens.

The architecture was timeless, a stoic façade of bleached, hewn stone, streaked and stained by time and minerals. The narrow stacks of gothic windows, their glass dark as water, climbed high along the walls, some reaching as high as the gables fifty feet up. A dozen or so chimneys rose from the ashy roof peaks, the crowns blackened by the decades. Men had labored to build this place long ago, maybe fifty or eighty years earlier, maybe longer. Looking at it, I thought of Europe, of the French countryside and of Rome. I had been to none of these places.

We reached a coral drive. "There," Abraham said, pointing toward an arched entryway.

"Through there?" I asked.

"Mmm."

I took this as an affirmation. Beyond him I could see a circular driveway, with steps leading up to a colonnade and what looked to be a recessed entrance. It seemed the more appropriate way.

Abraham tilted his head, interrupting my field of vision. His expression flat, he nodded again toward the narrow passage.

"Yes, thank you," I said, taking a deep breath.

Through the vaulted opening, I entered the tunnel, the wall on one side lined with a worn relief, men and women bearing tiny objects overhead, groaning beneath the weight. The other wall was smooth, the stone cool. I emerged at the other end, stepping off the granite slab into a pebbled courtyard.

It was a large enclosed quadrangle, neglected, overgrown with shrubbery and heavy gnarled brush. I noticed a high stone wall to my right, thick green vines climbing up and over it, and I could hear the dribbling of an unseen fountain somewhere in front of me. At the far end I could see patches of filmy green glass of what looked like a conservatory. A narrow path ran to my left and right, the foliage thick on either side of it.

Up and to my left hung a small second-story terrace, an elaborate iron lattice surrounding it, the door cracked an inch. Now I smelled it, the burn of a cigarette in the air.

I waited for a minute or two, stuck, then decided perhaps I was meant to keep moving. I followed the path to my right, pushing aside the brush as needed, a thorn branch snagging my sleeve, the track forking a couple of times. I continued until I came to a heavy, wooden door. I pressed down on the latch. It didn't give. I pulled at the thick handle, it was locked. I looked down at the basket beside the door. Lemons. I reached down and picked one up, turned it over in my hand, dropped it back.

Determined, I pushed on through the derelict hedgerows, ducking as necessary, until I found myself winding back around to my starting point. The trickle of water was still clear. I looked up and over my shoulder; the balcony door was now shut.

My anxiety rising, I sat down on a stone bench, the surface slimy with moss. My neck and jaw were now stiff. I noticed a ceramic pig tipped on its side a few feet away, and just beyond it lay a snake, half-exposed, its oily skin black and shiny against the dull rocks. I tossed a few pebbles at it. They all missed. A few minutes passed and my heartbeat slowed.

I was biting at a nail when I heard the whistling.

He came bouncing around the corner, a wide tray of flowered plants in hand, his face covered by a large floppy hat, and he was wearing a tan jumpsuit, a dark green smock tied around his waist.

Our eyes met, and he froze, his body at once rigid, his mind working quickly, analyzing, evaluating, and then, as if the pieces had all fallen into place, his face lit up.

"Oh, wow! Hey!" he said, shaking his head as if amused.

"Hello," I said, rising to my feet.

He swiveled back and forth, looking for a place to set the tray of flowers. Finally, he nodded at the bench, and I stepped aside. Hands free, he pulled off a glove and held out his hand.

"Hè! Kulamàlsi hàch?" he said.

"Pardon?" I said, shaking his hand.

"It's an Indian greeting—what they used to say around here maybe five hundred years ago, or so. Sorry if you were waiting long. Were you?"

"Huh?"

"Waiting long?" he asked, pulling back his sleeve to check his watch, a gold diver's model. "Oh, jeez. Time got away, so sorry."

"No, it's fine, it was only a couple minutes. I'm—. Well, I'm not so sure how to explain. I'm supposed to . . . do you know Abraham?"

"Big black guy?"

"He drove me here."

"Yeah, he treat you OK?"

"Fine, yes. I'm supposed to be meeting someone, and I'm not sure the best way to explain it."

The man started to laugh.

"Welcome to *Jardin des Connaissances,* my friend," he said, removing his hat and giving a mock bow. A golden mop of hair fell over his face, which was tanned, bright with perspiration. His nose was crooked, a bad break from when he was younger, I supposed. And he smelled skunky. I wondered if Robert Redford might have a less accomplished brother who'd taken up landscaping.

"I'm Marty," he said.

"Marty?"

"I'm glad you made it. It's Tom, right?" He had a toothy smile, with crow's feet clenching around his bright green eyes. "Sorry for all the cloak-and-dagger silliness, the secret code words and all, it's just I like to keep a low profile."

"I thought it was kind of cool," I said. "I felt like James Bond or something. 'For the end of the world,'" I said, repeating the phrase I'd been given to say.

"James Bond, right. That Roger Moore is so handsome. What was the last one, *The Man with the Golden Gun*? Great film."

"I didn't see that one," I said, realizing my heart was pounding hard against my chest.

"I know this place isn't much to look at just yet, Tom, but we're gonna get it whipped into shape, pronto. Total disaster when I got here, trust me. Belonged to this merchant prince department store fellow. Jameson was the name, I think. Jacobsen? He lost most everything way back in the depression, and the place went to total crud. By the time I bought it things were in pretty bad shape. Good price, though. C'mon, follow me."

He moved fast up the path, dodging a low branch, taking us right past the elusive fountain, around a corner and up to a set of glass doors, already ajar.

Before us was a vast, ruined foyer. A broad marble staircase, half collapsed, rising up and around to a second-floor gallery. Stale air, and yellow light seeping in through the dirty skylights high above, illuminating a galaxy of particulate suspended over us. Pink peony wallpaper, stained and bubbling, and the words EAT ME graffitied in red spray paint across a wall.

"This place was a real gem in its heyday. Really great parties," Marty said. "Imagine what some of these pieces would've been worth back in the day?"

A hoard of orphaned furniture. I wandered through the leftovers. A china cabinet on its side, its insides spilled across the discolored checkerboard tile. A pair of wooden, high-backed dining chairs, thick leather straps stemming from the seats, like something from a torture chamber. In the far corner sat a buffet table apparently fashioned after the Ark of the Covenant, resting atop a soiled Polar Bear rug.

"Hey, Tom, look at this."

I turned to see Marty, his head concealed by a black, helmet-like mask of Anubis, the Egyptian canine-god of the afterlife.

"I love playing with this stuff," he said, setting aside the mask and picking up a native American headdress, the generous plumes of red, black, white and a brilliant bubblegum blue radiating around his face, down alongside his shoulders.

I ran my finger along a giant armoire, a stripe in the dust. Several other pieces sat draped in cloth. Three oil landscapes leaned against a far wall, one of the canvases torn.

"Well . . ." I said, trying to think of how to finish my sentence.

"Tom," he said, "this world is falling apart. But I wanna show everyone what we can accomplish when the right people put their minds together and are willing to do a little bit of hard work."

He paused, pulling at an ancient peel of cracked green paint from the massive door he was standing beside. "These doors, they were originally from an old church in Europe. This ancient cathedral. Crazy, right? And look," he said, leaning into the massive door, pushing it open to reveal a long corridor. The ceiling of the passage vaulted upward into a brassy arcade, with glimmering blue light filtering through cathedral-style windows.

"Wow," I said.

"Yeah, and so here's the rest of the church, literally. The original architect used it as a hallway to connect the northern quarters to the southern quarters; had the whole thing dismantled and shipped over from Bucharest or some place."

"It looks restored?" I said.

"Yeah, we started here. And wait till you hear what we're gonna do with the pews."

The stark, white walls looked freshly painted. We walked the length of the passage until we reached the set of doors at the other end.

"And I really hope you like this," Marty said, grinning, pulling open the doors, revealing a golden atrium. The air in here was sweet and cool, fresh flowers spilling out of a dozen copper urns stationed around the room. A selection of landscapes from the Renaissance hung along the walls. Four marble pillars, one in each corner, rose high toward the ceiling, the faces of men and beasts carved into their crowns. And, higher still, the chandeliers were aglow, casting soft light on the dark celestial beings painted on the ceiling above them. My eyes drifted over to the windows, long and rectangular, running from the ceiling all the way down to a ledge, thigh high, linen drapes swaying softly, the breezy, autumn air pushing through.

I began to laugh.

"What is it?" Marty asked, head tilted.

"It's so beautiful," I said. "I would have never expected it."

My comment pleased him.

"I'm an old soul, I suppose," he said. "One day, Tom, it will all be restored. All things new."

I put my hand to the cold, stone bosom of a life-size sculpture, a man with a book and a staff.

"One of the saints?" I asked, knowing he would say yes.

Marty looked at the statue, then back at me, almost puzzled. "Ah, no. Please, over here. Let's find a seat."

He led me toward a pair of crimson chairs in a corner nook. I sank into the soft leather, craning my neck up to once again try and capture the height of the room. My heart stirred.

"I have something for us," Marty said, disappearing momentarily into an alcove, reappearing with a glass of wine and a cheese platter.

"Here you are, sir. The Swiss Gruyère is divine," he said. "I'm embarrassed to ask, but would you ever forgive me if I just borrow a quick moment to freshen up?"

I raised my glass. "Take your time."

He put his hands together and bowed, then hurried off in a mock run, making a silly face at me as he rounded the corner.

I took a sip of the Cabernet, smooth, but substantial. I tried the Gouda, the Camembert, the Brie. The warmth of the wine was soon washing over me, inspiring me to explore.

On my feet again, I wandered over to the row of windows, looking out at the magnificent view of the back of the property and the river below. There was a raised stone pavilion, ringed with Greek columns that overlooked an algae-skinned pool. The colonnade was surrounded by a garden, half manicured, which then led out to a patchy lawn of ancient oaks. From here the elevation sloped gently down toward the Hudson, dark and indifferent.

To the south were three giant satellite dishes, pointed toward the sky, and then, immediately, I knew I understood. The trees were beginning to sway, the wind was picking up, and a drizzle was beginning to speck the glass. I stood there in a trance, watching the weather deteriorate.

Then I heard his voice again.

I turned as Marty approached, his wet hair combed back, looking handsome in a mustard turtleneck, brown slacks and loafers.

"How's that cheese?" he asked, waving me back toward the chairs.

"Delicious."

"Oh, goodie." He took a bite. "Mmm, I have to say, I was so sorry to hear about Professor Kruppold."

"Yeah," I said. "He lived a lot of years."

"But that was quite a way to go," Marty said, wincing. "Unfortunate."

"I don't think I heard the specifics?" I said.

"My understanding is they tried to keep the details out of the papers. Gruesome, really. Random, the police said. Probably some uneducated hooligans. They tore him up pretty good. Made a real mess."

"I had no idea," I said.

"Kitchen knives, I heard. And he lived in such a nice neighborhood, too. Cute house, right there by the university. Little birdhouse out front, painted green and yellow."

"Lock your doors, I guess," I said.

"And that's the crazy part, Tom," Marty said, taking a quick sip of wine. "The police said no signs of forced entry. Like he just opened up the front door, let them in. He was such a kind, trusting man."

"Gosh, I really wasn't aware of the details," I said, giving him a quick smile.

"Leave those to Patti, right? She's the journalist? She doing OK with her transition from academia?"

"Pretty well. I didn't realize you— How exactly did you know about that?"

"Trailblazing Patti? Well, she's practically a celebrity now. *Newsweek*'s a really big deal."

"Sure," I said, leaning back in my chair.

"But you're the one who's got the questions, right?"

"Right, yes," I said. "But before we start, Marty, I want to make sure you know I don't mean any harm."

"Harm?" he said, laughing, spreading his arms wide before bringing his glass back close for another sip. "Oh, gosh, I thought we were just going to have a conversation."

"No, that's not what I mean. I didn't . . ."

"Tom, listen to me. I believe you're here for a reason, right?"

"Yes," I said.

"Your particular faith path hasn't been easy, has it?"

"No, I suppose not."

"Tell me about it."

"I was always fascinated by church: the stories, the way our priest made them sound heroic, almost mythical. Good versus evil, weak versus strong, life versus death. Even as a little boy I'd read the scriptures and ask questions. My mother didn't know what to do with me. She sent me to talk to our priest, Father Parry. I'm sure he was amused, this little kid asking him about the mark of the beast and the four horsemen of the apocalypse."

Marty smiled. "And I'm glad you're here, Tom. Providence, I like to say. And so this Professor Kruppold told you some things at a party, a few years back, right? But then he got cold feet, said *pretend you never heard any of that*? And then later he sent you a note? With my name and my address."

"Right, like I said in the letter I sent you back in June. He said he served with you on the USS *Maine*."

"Oh, goodness, here we go."

"During the Spanish–American War," I said.

"Seems silly, doesn't it?"

"In 1898—seventy-eight years ago." My voice cracked saying this.

"Tell me more," Marty said, his tone dropping, leaning forward in his chair, chin dropping into palm. "This is getting interesting."

"Kruppold said he was fifteen at the time, and you were middle-aged, about forty or so. You were both aboard a naval vessel, the USS *Maine,* the night she exploded in Havana. He survived with injuries, but you were among the nearly three hundred sailors lost. You had been a chaplain aboard the ship."

"Go on."

"He said he never forgot you. I guess you had been a real encouragement to him. He'd been homesick."

Marty seemed to enjoy this detail.

"Which," I continued, nearly out of breath now, "is why he was so surprised to run into you with his stepdaughter at a restaurant nearly fifty years later."

"Sylvia," Marty said. "Nice girl. She loved to fish, I remember."

"It's true?" I asked.

"Oh, yes, that girl was nuts for fishing. Kind of gets to be a little too much at a certain point, you know? Fish for lunch, fish for dinner, fishing every weekend. I'm more of a meat-and-potatoes guy, you know""

"What?"

"Just being silly, Tom. Is it true, you ask? The story Kruppold told you? Well, you wouldn't have come all this way if you weren't already a believer, right?"

"Right, and?" I asked.

"And I don't suppose I can deny it. I read your letter, the pieces you've put together. That's what you do, right? Help put things together. You're an engineer? What kind again?"

"Civil."

"That makes sense. I find you to be very civil. And we could use a good engineer around here. But I also believe you're so much more than an engineer, Tom. There's something about you, a depth. You strike me as different, someone who sees a bigger picture? Actually, you know, it's a relief to have someone to talk to about all this. It's not easy."

"And is the story of the doomed bomber true?" I asked, almost giddy now. "You saved all those men and then walked away from the crash unharmed?"

"Everybody loves a war hero."

"Does Abraham know?"

Marty looked around the room, lowering his voice. "Abraham is a nice young man with some financial needs. Right now his primary concern is becoming the next Sergio Oliva."

"Who?"

"Well, that's exactly what I said. But Abraham did place sixth in the Mr. Galaxy competition last summer. Very proud day around here."

"Is he OK? He seems pretty spaced out?"

"I've got big plans for him. It's not a short story, how I found him, gave him his new name, everything I asked him to do, what he left behind," Marty said, appearing to drift off for a moment before snapping back. "So tell me, Tom, who is it that you think that I am?"

"I know who you are. Professor Kruppold told me."

"OK."

"After years of research he finally got it."

"And? C'mon, the suspense is killing me."

"You're real name is John."

Marty sat up in his seat, his eyes narrowed, locking in on mine. "Go on."

I took a deep breath. "You are John the Apostle, immortal, alive after nearly two thousand years."

A door slammed in the distance. Marty jerked his head back and around. There were footsteps approaching, soft but determined. A girl in a yellow bikini appeared around the corner.

"Rebecca," Marty said. "Hey, this is my friend Tom."

"There's beetles in the pool again," she said. "It's disgusting."

"Again?" he called back to her. "What about the other pool, the outside pool?"

"It's raining."

"Well, it is a pool, sweetie. A great big hole filled with water. What's a little rain?"

"It's October," she said.

"Caviar troubles," Marty whispered to me with a what-can-you-do smile.

"I'll call someone to come take a looksie, dear," he called back to her.

She stood there for a moment, pouty, then shrugged and slinked away.

Marty stood, wine glass in hand.

"Poor thing. But she's a very nice girl. Reminds me of her Great Aunt Helen. Come and see, we'll have more privacy this way."

We slipped through a small door leading to a spiral staircase, climbing up, up, around, and down a narrow hall and into a wide mahogany-paneled study.

"This is where I like to do my thinking," Marty said.

A balcony ran the length of the room, and the shelved walls of both floors were crammed with books. There were half a dozen wooden tables, a pair of leather couches and a few chairs. The floor-to-ceiling windows at the east end overlooked the grounds.

Marty moved along the shelves, searching and selecting, the books piling up in his arms. He scattered them across one of the tables.

"Here, let me show you something," he said.

Their covers read as follows:

Revelation   **Revelación**   **Révélation**   **Rivelazione**

Apocalipsis   **Αποκάλυψη**

Offenbarung   **תולגתה**   **Апокалипсис**   **啟示录**

الكشف   **黙示録**   **انكشافات**

"Apokalupsis," he said, holding up another. "Still my favorite. The original Greek. I've read them all, though. Tell me, what do you think it's like, Tom? To be alive two thousand years?"

"I can't imagine," I said, my heart and mind racing.

"Seven hundred thousand sunrises, give or take. Seven hundred thousand sunsets. Not that you catch them all. I circled the globe a dozen times before the first airplanes. I was one of the first white men to breathe the virgin air of North America."

"1649," I said. "I read your journal. Kruppold had it."

"Speaking of which, did you know people were already settled and living here fifteen thousand years ago?"

"Really?" I said.

"I suppose. I think I read that in a book somewhere. I've read a lot of books. I even wrote a few."

"Your work's very important," I said. "Still spreading the good news, I'm sure?"

Marty smiled. "I've made love to the most beautiful women in the world. And their daughters. And their granddaughters. I've saved men in battle only to take their grandsons' lives a generation later."

"Wait, what?" I asked.

"Well, Tom, I mean I'm only human. There was only one perfect man to walk this earth, and he ain't me."

I leaned forward, enthralled.

"You want to know, don't you?" he said, almost a whisper. "There were countless messiahs in those days, each promising their own flavor of freedom. And those people, the masses, they were desperate, wandering out into the desert to find these guys, eager for the hope they were selling: freedom, autonomy, identity. And the

Romans crushed them all, grinding their legacies to dust, their names all forgotten, except one."

"The Christ?" I said.

"That's right. And I knew him."

"Were you there. At the end?"

"The end? You mean the day man killed GOD? That's something you can't forget. The sky goes black, the whole earth shakes, and pretty much all heck breaks loose. Meanwhile, it's happening, on an obscure, filthy little hill, just a handful of soldiers, the women watching, crumpled in sorrow along with his mother and, of course, that beloved apostle whom you spoke of earlier."

"And what of— Wait, who?" I asked.

"The beloved disciple, John," he said.

"But I thought— I guess I'm confused?"

"John the Apostle, author of the fourth gospel, brother of James the martyr, son of Zebedee, message bearer of Christ and an enemy of the Roman Empire, survivor of execution by boiling oil, and banished to the Isle of Patmos, where he penned the Revelation.

"Raised in a dirty little town near Bethsaida. Had this wild, curly black hair, best I can recall anyway. Hell, what do I know; I only saw him once. This man, rumored by some to be immortal, did in fact live to be nearly one hundred years old, a real feat. But, sadly, he is dead, and has been for almost nineteen centuries."

I licked my lips. My mouth was dry.

"I was trained as a physician. My skills were sharp, and eventually I found myself in the house of Pontius Pilate. Ever hear of him? Don't you want to know what he looked like? Burt Lancaster, maybe? Unfortunately, I can't recall. Anyhow, I was privy to the movements of various popular figures in the region. I'd heard the rumors and, of course, wanted to see for myself. And I did. I watched him make a sick woman whole. That was neat. I saw him open the eyes of a child supposedly blind since birth. Also neat. All joking aside, his powers amazed me." Marty paused, watching me closely. "You OK?"

I nodded.

"You see, Tom, just like you, I had a son. His name was Anastasias. He was a beautiful boy: smart, funny, sweet personality. Beautiful kid, olive skin, green eyes. He was six when it happened. The illness. Terrible fevers. But with all my wisdom and all my skill I couldn't help him. He fell into a coma. My wife and I were desperate. It took me two days, but finally, on the second night I tracked the teacher down in a camp twenty miles outside the city."

"What happened?" I asked.

"I asked for his help."

"And?"

"And the teacher, he looked at me and he smiled and said, 'Take comfort, friend, for tonight the boy is with his Father in Heaven.'"

Marty let this sentence hang for a moment.

"I see the look on your face, Tom. And yes, that's right, my boy died."

"Oh. I'm sorry."

"Shocking, right? This coming from the guy who'd been so eager to help every bum, beggar and whore in all of white trash Galilee, but somehow it's better if my son dies? I was angry, Tom. Furious. I told him, 'If you were the son of God, you'd take away these people's suffering. You'd erase death. You'd overthrow this Empire and bring peace to this world.' Then I spit at him. In his face. Got him right here. He didn't flinch. Tough dude, for sure. He just looks back at me with these injured eyes, and finally he says, 'Is that what you would do?'"

"'Yes,' I told him. 'I'd fix it, your creation. I'd fix the things you won't.'" And then he nodded and said, 'If my Father allows, that Power will be yours. And so it will be for a season.' Weird, right? The words meant nothing to me, and I left him, furious. A few days later I buried my son, did my best to move on, although I found it impossible."

"I'm not really sure what to say, Marty."

"It's OK. I realize it's heavy. Probably unfair for me to just dump all that on you. Hey, here's the story of how my kid died and Jesus didn't give me what I asked for."

"But, Marty, your story—" I stopped myself.

"What?" Marty asked. "What were you going to say?"

"That story, about the physician, you and your son. I don't mean any disrespect, but that story's not anywhere in the Bible."

"I know that," Marty said.

"So?" I asked.

"So, what? Geez, Tom, there's lots of things not in the Bible. It even says that in the Bible. It's even like, hey, there's lots of other things that happened, a whole bunch of other things, but those stories aren't all in here."

"Right, OK."

"So you tell me, Tom. You're a father. What was wrong with me wanting my son to live?"

"I don't know," I said.

"You don't know, like you're unsure? Or you don't know, like you agree with me?"

I stammered, not sure how to feel or respond.

"Doesn't matter," Marty said. "Anyhow, a few months later I sat there, watching him die. Just like the story, a cross, a dirty hill, a terrifying storm. Scared the crud out of everybody within fifty miles no doubt. And it didn't bring me any peace to see that. Then later, of course, there were the rumors of, well, you know, and that's when the movement really took off. I guess I should've bought stock.

"Three years later our ship sank off the coast of Crete. My wife and two daughters were lost at sea, along with the rest on board. I was adrift in the Mediterranean, no food, no fresh water. Day after day, sun and sharks, they literally ate the clothes off me. Three weeks later I washed ashore on a mostly deserted island, naked and hungry, but otherwise intact. They called it Perellia, or something like that. The locals entertained me briefly before I made my way to Rome."

Marty looked back over the spread of books on the table, taking one into his hands.

"You asked me who I am, Tom. Do you still want to know?"

"Yes," I said, bracing myself.

"I'm not who you or Professor Kruppold thought. I'm not John. But, coincidentally, I am the subject of John's writing." He tapped his finger on one of the books before him. "I'm the one who will one day set the world free: free from war, free from disease, free from death and, most importantly, free from him." He pointed his index finger up toward the ceiling.

I thought about what he was saying, connecting the dots. My whole body went cold.

"Go on, Tom. Say it."

I tried to force the words out. "You are . . ."

"You can do it."

"Antichrist?"

"Ooh," he said, wincing, bringing his hands up in defense. "I really don't like that label. My name's Marty. And besides, the word "anti" is so negative. I'm about the positive, making things better, that sort of thing."

"I don't understand," I said, trembling, looking around the room, first toward the door, next to see if there was any kind of object I might use against him. "But what about the heroic war story?" I asked

"What about it, friend? Don't you get it? I'm not the enemy. I'm not the Lucifer. I despise him. His goal is to destroy mankind. My goal is to save us."

"What do you mean?"

"Let God and the devil go duke it out somewhere else, leave us in peace. Let us work together to solve the real problems. Cancer, pollution, genocide, poverty: these are all abominations that undermine our human race.

"The latest advances in science and medicine are unprecedented. Soon a man will no longer submit to the scourge of old age, he'll never have to watch his lover wrestle disease, and soon a father will never again have to bury a child. Your boy's name is Wade, right?"

"Yes," I said.

"How old?"

"Three," I said.

"A child is— How do we even place a value?"

"When will all of this happen? Everything in the books?" I asked, looking over at a reading lamp on the table beside me. I wondered if I could swing it hard enough to kill him.

"Tom, you look upset. Have I upset you?"

"It's a lot of information to handle, Marty."

"You're right. I'm sorry for that. I didn't mean to trouble you. You know, there's a pride within me I have to tether."

"A pride?"

"Scripture is full of language suggesting it was imminent in the first century. Had I not caught myself, I would've soon found myself Emperor of Rome. On six occasions my pride has nearly gotten the best of me, and only at the last moment did I course correct, throwing myself back into the shadows. Would you know a great man of history if he stood before you: a philosopher, a pope, a king, a great explorer?"

"I don't know."

"I was a confidant of Roosevelt's. I'd been with him since New York. When FDR ran for his third term he shortlisted me for his vice president. I declined, and he chose Wallace. Of course, had I been VP, I would've convinced Roosevelt to avoid the war."

"So Hitler could take over the world?"

"Conventional wisdom, that Hitler could've accomplished something like that, but Hitler didn't have the depth. America would've survived. The oceans protect us. Hitler would've decimated Europe and, more importantly, Russia. FDR would've died in the spring of forty-five, and, assuming FDR had kept me on instead of Truman, I'd have become president of the United States, at which time I would have led America in a rise to crush Hitler, thereby delivering the entire world from a Nazi regime."

"But Hitler was evil. I don't follow."

"Tom, why're you so hung up on this idea that I'm a bad guy? Hello, my name is Marty *Goode*, not Marty *Bad*. I'm here to save the world from the bad guys. And people will be thankful, devoted. A long time ago people thought that the Roman emperors were the, you know, that word you like to use . . ."

"Antichrist."

"Yeah, because of the visceral attacks on Christianity and the destruction of Jerusalem and the Temple, just like it had been predicted. There were five emperors in a very short period; the whole world was in chaos. In all the excitement I came very close to taking charge of the operation, and had that occurred, I would've brought order and peace to the Empire, and to the entire world. What's so bad about that?"

"But you didn't."

"I've always been fortunate enough to sense him, waiting, right there at my elbow."

"Who?" I asked.

Marty looked at me, clenching his jaw.

"But eventually, it'll happen?" I said.

"Tom, I could free the nations. And they would embrace me. Even the churchgoers, yes, especially them. Who wouldn't prefer a life of health and success over a Heaven that takes dying to reach? If I was revealed, the world would stand in awe of a man who could not die. Their eyes would open, and they'd crave my leadership, begging for a change from the old ways, the same old lunacy of the President Fords and the Secretary Brezhnevs. No more sickness and poverty and petty religion.

"Imagine a world of health and abundance and peace and, you know, there's always going to be those who don't like it, those who fear it, try to destroy it. But they'd fail. Because for the first time in history all the armies of the world would be united, able to keep the peace and stop anyone who threatens what we'd have built. And, finally, the people would be free."

"And what about the rest of the story?"

"Hmm?"

I pointed to the books.

He nodded.

"There would be those who reject my gift, the ones who would actually choose death over life. It's sad. I mean, what are you gonna do? You can't stop them, right? And so I suppose that'd be what they got. Very sad."

"And with their final breaths," I said, straightening up, feeling emboldened, "they will look to the east and whisper, 'Come, Lord Jesus, come.' And He will hear their voice. And He will summon the armies of Heaven, a hundred billion angels, into war. Creation at war with Creator, the earth will shake and the sky will collapse, and mountains will be cast into the sea. Fire will fall, billions will perish, and the moon will be red like blood.

Then, at your command, the dead will rise to join the fight, and in that moment, in your desperation, you will form an unholy alliance and allow the Lucifer what he's always desired, the ability to inhabit human form, and together you will lead the final charge against Christ on behalf of all mankind."

Marty sat there in silence, eyes narrowed, leaning against the table, watching me. Finally, he spoke.

"Is that what it really says?"

"Yes," I said. "More or less, that's the scholarly interpretation."

"Are you sure?" he asked.

"What?" I said.

"How old were you, Tom, when you realized your dreams would not come true? You didn't last very long in seminary, did you? What was it, a semester?"

"Two semesters," I said, feeling a heat in my ears and face.

"Two," Marty repeated. "Why? I mean, why didn't you finish?"

"Patti convinced me. She said it was just somebody else pushing their life on me. She said I was too gullible."

"Patti. She's always been very influential on you. Trust me, I understand why. She's a smart girl. But I want you to know, Tom, I see your potential. I believe in you. I believe in your talent, your intellect. Will you believe in me?"

"You're on the losing side," I said. "You can't win."

"Am I? I mean, you're right, that's one interpretation. But remember, John was biased and, don't forget, almost a hundred when he wrote all that. The brain gets squishy."

"It's scripture. It's divinely inspired."

"Just because you read something in a book doesn't make it true, does it?"

"You seem uneasy," I said.

He turned and walked over to the corner of the study and, for the first time, I noticed it: a large dog lying atop a red sleeping bag. Marty kneeled, running his hand along the fur.

"You like dogs, Tom? I've always loved dogs. All animals, really, but dogs, they're such beautiful creatures. Her name is Karla. I rescued her when she was a pup. She's almost eleven now. Her kidneys are failing. I'm losing her. Maybe tonight."

"She's a German shepherd?" I asked.

"A wolf, actually. I'm sure it's easy to judge, Tom, but you don't know what it's like—to lose them all? Everyone you've ever known, everyone you've ever loved? Family, friends, even pets. I'm only human."

"Right," I said.

"Over and over, again and again. Lovers, beautiful and delicious, only to spoil like fruit. Why is it wrong that I want to change that?"

"You're certainly ambitious."

"Enough with your snide remarks. How easy you all have it. What a paradise it would be to lead a simple existence, to lack ambition, passing through history unseen, the bliss of wasting your lives on cigarettes and bingo."

He put his face down beside the animal, whispering to her. Then he stood back up, wiping at his eyes, walking past me toward the window. The weather had worsened. The rain was heavy, obscuring the river, its waters whitecapping.

"You know, with the right balance, we can draw this out indefinitely, with good people, men and women with skills. You would be happy here. Patti could come, too. And Wade. The quarters are nice; there's a bowling alley, swimming pools."

"With beetles," I said. "I can't believe the antichrist is trying to seduce me with a bowling alley."

"The south wing has a bunker two hundred feet deep. We built that first, in case of nuclear attack. And next year we're adding a movie theater. That's where we're putting the pews, from that old church in Europe? In the movie theater. Here, let me show you the plans. I bet with your background you'd have some great ideas for us. And I have friends, contacts in Hollywood. I bet we could get the whole James Bond collection here, just for you."

"Marty," I said.

"Huh?"

"I should go."

"Go?"

"Patti doesn't even know I'm here, and it's getting late."

With this I had wounded him. I saw the look of a child whose hurt shifts slowly into contempt. His eyes narrowed, his lips were pursed. Then he nodded, slowly, his face returning to neutral, and then a smile.

"I understand, Tom. I get it. You've got a family, a big responsibility. No hard feelings. Thanks for spending your day with me. I enjoyed talking with you."

"Thank you, Marty."

"But," he added, grinning, "there's always time, you know, in case you ever changed your mind. If you do, you'll give me a jingle?"

WHILE I NEVER SHARED THE STORY of my visit with Marty with Patti, I would eventually tell Wade and his friends The Tale of Mr. Young (that's what I would call it, and yes, I know it's not that creative) as they sat wide-eyed, eager to hear about the man who never died. "Again, Dad, tell it again. "And I never forgot Marty, his hospitality, his enthusiasm, his idealism.

And while my fascination with Marty and the stories that led me to him never lost their intrigue, ultimately I resolved to let it go, accepting in the end that it was all the work of randomness, that Marty was little more than an eccentric screwball with a great imagination, some level of financial independence, and endless charisma.

To put it more bluntly, Marty was nuts. Kruppold was just as nuts, maybe even more so, and truthfully, it was easier to just let it all go. And so I moved on.

LIFE PASSES QUICKLY. You wake up one day, and your little boy is a man. You catch the reflection of an old person in a store-front window, and the old person is you.

Our lives were good ones. We enjoyed successful careers, the pleasure of great friends, private school for Wade, a home in the country club. In the early 2000s we retired well, we traveled, vacationed in London, saw France and Italy. We watched with pride as Wade established his own life, his own career, first in finance, then, after the layoffs of 2008, an eventual reboot into real estate. Thanksgivings with him in New York City became our new family tradition.

One Sunday afternoon in May of 2013 Patti was crossing the parking lot of a Super Target when she collapsed. By the time the paramedics arrived she was gone. A heart attack. She was only sixty-nine. My best friend. The loss was sudden, immeasurable and final. Untethered, I found myself disoriented, adrift.

LATE NOVEMBER 2013

W E ARE CLOSE.

"Turn right in five hundred feet," the GPS tells us. Wade begins to brake. I can't believe we're here.

The road leading into the trees is now paved smooth, the battered gates are gone, allowing us to progress quickly, although the wood feels no less haunted.

Now we can see it ahead, the growth is expansive, the main estate along with several new structures, also classic in architecture, two and three stories tall, constructed to maintain a uniform style across the grounds.

"An athletic facility, stables, and, get this, an armory," Wade says. "Sixty-five million dollars. It goes on the market tomorrow. There's even a landing pad out back. Whoever buys it will probably chopper into the city each day."

"This is your listing?" I ask.

"I wish. The agency principal is handling it, but I wanted you to see it."

"Why's the owner selling it?"

"I don't know. Who knows with these billionaires. Maybe he went bust. Or maybe he's just bored and wants something different."

Wade pulls around the circle drive and eases to a stop. I glance up at the house, still in disbelief.

"Who is he?" I ask. "The seller?"

Wade flips open the file.

"It's held by an LLC, which is typical, but I'm pretty sure. Let's see. I know there's a name listed. Here, no wait." He continues to scan down the pages. "Here it is. His name is Titus Peppering. I think someone in the office said he's relocating to Hong Kong or something. You ready?"

"Ready?" I ask.

"To check it out," Wade says. "C'mon, let's go inside."

Climbing out of the car, it feels good to take a moment to stretch. And then as we're walking across the pea-gravel drive, he says it. . .

"It reminds me of that story you'd tell us when I was little, the one about the goofball guy who was like a thousand years old?"

WADE OPENS UP THE MAIN HOUSE, and we spend the next hour exploring. The atrium, the library study, they are just as I remembered, although the books are gone. The ballrooms, the dozens of guest quarters, the three kitchens. Eventually we even find the bowling alley, just down the hall from the movie theater. It's all updated, just like new.

Exploring room to room, I pull out my phone and Google "Titus Peppering." He is a multinational businessman in his mid-fifties, plump round face, dark hair. Wade looks over as I laugh out loud.

"What is it, Dad?"

"I'm just laughing at myself."

To think I could've actually considered it; to think I had actually believed it was possible.

Walking back out to the car I take a guess about the seller. "I bet a guy this rich is probably a real jerk. Maybe it's good it's not your listing, son. That way you don't have to deal with him."

"He actually stopped by the office on Monday."

"Who?" I ask.

"The seller. All the ladies were talking about it, said he was this blonde-headed, surfer-looking guy, really nice to everyone, super laid back."

"Titus Peppering?" I ask as I pull my door shut.

"Yeah," Wade says, buckling his seatbelt and picking the file back up.

"You met him?" I ask.

"No, I was out on an appointment. OK, wait. Sorry, here it is. I guess Peppering is just the trustee. Sorry about that. But the owner, here it is, his name's listed right here."

His index finger is pointing to a line on the page as he hands me the file, and there it is, typed out plainly, the name "Marty Goode."

I turn away from it. I am in shock, dazed, and my mind feels disconnected from my body, from reality. I look out the passenger window, the meticulous landscaping, the ivory stone, the dark windows. I feel the paper in my hands, begin to fold it carefully, over and over, my hands beginning to shake, again and again, forming smaller and smaller rectangles, tucking it in my shirt pocket.

"You alright, Dad?"

"Yes, I'm OK." And then I say, "They really fly by, don't they, son?"

"What?"

"The years. It all goes so fast."

A light snow is beginning to fall as we ease away, rounding the circle drive, into the thick of trees, and soon back onto the main road.

The trip back to the city is beautiful. We talk about things: Wade's memories of when he was younger; favorite times with his mom; how much we both miss her; how we wish she was still here; how it doesn't quite make sense.

Then Wade says it: "I guess you just never know how much time's left, you know, to make the most of things."

I put my hand to my chest, the folded piece of paper near my heart. Soon we will reach Wade's apartment, have a nice holiday meal, watch the games. And then at some point, I will excuse myself, closing the door to my room, taking a seat in the chair beside the window, the Hudson heavy and dark beyond the pane, and I will unfold the page, smoothing the creases with care, rubbing the tip of my finger across the name, that special name, Marty Goode, with the phone number beside it. Lifting the receiver, I will dial, it will ring, and he will answer.

I can hear his voice now, the pep in his hello, that everlasting charm. And I will identify myself, remind him of our afternoon together, and let him know:

I'm finally ready, old friend.
Please, tell me, how can I help?

With deepest gratitude: to my girls, Dusty and London, for their endless support; to John Dufresne, Kim Bradley, and the Seaside crew of Fall 2014 (Jim, Jennifer, Liz, Karina, Robin, and Stephanie) for their feedback and ideas; to my parents; to Rita; to my man MM; to Kassie who pushed me forward; to my feedback readers, Jordan, Melissa, Julia, and Megan; to my copyeditor, Peter Guess; and to you, my reader. Thank you.

If you enjoyed this story, please share with friends, which will allow me to share more stories in the future.